T3-BHD-773

Good Morning, Strawbery Banke

Written and Illustrated by Wickie Rowland

PW

PublishingWorks, Inc.
2010

Copyright © 2010 by Strawbery Banke Museum.
All rights reserved. No part of this book may be reproduced or transmitted in any form or by any means, electronic or mechanical, including photocopying, recording, or by an information storage and retrieval system— except by a reviewer who may quote brief passages in a review to be printed in a magazine or newspaper— without permission in writing from the publisher.

PublishingWorks, Inc.,
151 Epping Road
Exeter, NH 03833
603-778-9883

For Sales and Orders:
1-800-738-6603 or 603-772-7200

Design by: Anna Pearlman

LCCN: 2010904215
ISBN-13: 978-1-935557-62-3

Printed on recycled paper.
Printed in Canada.

Manufactured by Friesens Corp, Altona, MB, Canada, April 2010, job #54631

For Rodney, with love and thanks for all his encouragement and support, and for Larry, without whose perseverance and confidence, my portfolio would be empty.

Good Morning, J.D.! What is happening at Strawbery Banke?

Mr. Sherburne
is going to his
wharf where he
will count the
supplies that have
just come by ship
from England.

1783

Mrs. Wheelwright
is making a
pumpkin pie for
her family to eat
after dinner.

3

1789

Mrs. Stavers is cooking turkeys in honor of a special visit to the tavern by George Washington.

4

1795

Mr. Shapley and
his daughters
are counting the
sugar loaves to
make sure they
have plenty to sell
in their store.

1796

Dr. Jackson is
picking herbs
to make into
medicines for his
patients.

1805

Mr. Chase is
having a cup of
tea before he
starts another
busy day working
in his store.

Widow Mary Rider is busy paying bills before making breakfast for her nieces and nephews.

1850

Thomas Bailey Aldrich is sick in bed, counting the birds on his wallpaper.

9

Mrs. Goodwin
is busy working
in her garden,
planting all her
favorite flowers.

1919

Mrs. Shapiro is setting the table for her family's Sabbath meal.

11

Bertha Abbott is filling an order of bread and SPAM for an early customer.

Mrs. Pecunies is working in her Victory Garden, picking tomatoes to can for the winter.

1952

Mrs. Pridham is watching a new show called *The Today Show* on television before she starts her housework.

The Cooper is
making a barrel
like the ones that
used to be filled
with salted fish
and sent across
the ocean.

15

What are YOU
going to do today,
J.D.?

16

Can you find these items in this book?

Bake oven: There were no wall ovens in the 1700's so they used bake ovens, which were small holes inside the fireplace, to bake bread. A fire would be built inside to heat up the space, and then taken out and the bread dough put in to bake. Yum!

Dried fruit: Since there were no refrigerators in the 1780's, fruit was dried so that it would keep. Drying fruit was often a job done by children who would slice the fruit and hang it by the fire to dry.

Clock-jack: To cook things on a spit and have them cook evenly, the food would have to be turned constantly. This would be a boring job for someone unless you had a clock-jack, as Mrs. Stavers had. She could wind it and it would turn the spit for her so that she could do something else.

Sugar Loaf: White sugar was very expensive in 1795, and was only used for special occasions. The cones were solid and you had to grate them to be able to use the sugar. The blue paper that they were wrapped in was dyed blue with indigo, so you could soak the paper in water and dye clothes when you were finished with the sugar.

Tea Strainer: Until 1904, tea did not come in bags. You would put the tea leaves into the teapot, add hot water, and then pour the tea through a strainer so that you wouldn't get tea leaves floating in your cup.

Teapot: Tea was served to visitors and was an important part of doing business. If you went to visit a friend, they would always offer you tea. The strawberry pattern on Mrs. Rider's teapot was found on pieces of china that were dug up by Strawbery Banke archaeologists.

Wallpaper: When Thomas Bailey Aldrich grew up, he wrote a book called *The Story of a Bad Boy*, about his time in Portsmouth. Here is what he wrote about counting the birds on his wallpaper: "There were two hundred and sixty-eight of these birds in all, not counting those split in two where the paper joined . . . and falling asleep (I) immediately dreamed that the whole flock suddenly took wing and flew out the window."

Samovar: Mrs. Shapiro's samovar came from Russia. It was used to make a special, sweet tea which would be served to visitors.

Cheerioats: In the early 1940's Cheerios were called Cheerioats. The name was changed to Cheerios in 1946. In 1943, a box of Cheerioats cost 13 cents!

SPAM: SPAM was first sold in 1937. It was a meat made of pork shoulder and ham, and because it was sold in a can, it would keep fresh for a long time. Over 100 million pounds of SPAM were shipped overseas to the Allied troops during World War II.

Victory Garden: During World War II, lots of people grew vegetables in their back yards. This let the farmers send their own vegetables overseas to help feed the Allied soldiers fighting in the war.

Television: Television sets in the 1950's could only show black and white pictures. Color televisions hadn't been invented yet. Only 12 channels were available, but most televisions only got 3 or 4, and there were no remotes. If you wanted to change the channel or make it louder, you would have to get up and turn one of the knobs on the front of the television.

About J.D.

J.D. is a real, live cat who lives with his loving family—Mary & David, and another cat, Murphy—just a dash across the street and hop over the fence from the Goodwin House at Strawbery Banke. J.D. was abandoned on the streets of Seabrook, NH when he was about 2 years old. In 2004, David & Mary chose him from among all the other cats at the Stratham NHSPCA because he seemed friendly and confident. If you go to Strawbery Banke in the summertime, you'll probably see him.

Kids' Bank

At Piscataqua Savings Bank

This book was made possible by a generous donation from Piscataqua Savings Bank. The Bank, established in 1877, shares a strong place in local history with Strawbery Banke Museum. Piscataqua Savings is proud to collaborate on this special project and invites you to visit their Kids' Bank, dedicated to teaching children the value of saving and financial responsibility. Visit Portsmouth's Local Bank on Pleasant Street and meet the Kids' Bank bear mascot, B.A. Saver. Find fun activity sheets in the Kids' Bank area at www.piscataqua.com.

About the Author

Wickie Rowland (whose name, before you ask, comes from her middle name, Chadwick) has been drawing ever since she was old enough to hold a pencil. She has been involved with Strawbery Banke ever since she worked there as an interpreter while in college. She enjoys gardening, learning languages, traveling, and spending time with her family.

STRAWBERY BANKE PORTSMOUTH NEW HAMPSHIRE

The museum's name comes from the original name of Portsmouth, NH given by the settlers who discovered strawberries growing on the banks of the river. The settlers also created the unusual spelling of Strawbery Banke.

History Happened Here. For more than 300 years, people lived and worked in this waterfront neighborhood. At Strawbery Banke Museum you can experience how they lived, from 1695 to 1950. Through restored furnished houses, exhibits, period gardens, historic landscapes, costumed role players and guides, Strawbery Banke interprets the living history of the generations who settled in Portsmouth, NH.

For more information, visit www.StrawberyBanke.org

or call 603-433-1100.